# MY SECRET CRUSH

## A HOT LESBIAN ROMANCE

### REBA BALE

**MY SECRET CRUSH**

# CONTENTS

# ABOUT THIS BOOK

They're destined to love each other from afar, until their worlds collide...

Barista Camille has a secret: she's got a crush. An all-encompassing crush on the glamorous older woman who comes into her coffee shop every single day at precisely seven thirty a.m. It's crazy. Madison doesn't even know she's alive, but that doesn't keep Camille from dreaming about her every night.

Billionaire Madison has the weight of the world on her shoulders. The CEO of one of Seattle's largest software firms doesn't have time for dating, fun, or any type of a personal life. Too many people are depending on her. Yet every day she finds herself lingering at the Morning Jolt coffee shop, flirting with Camille while waiting for her daily cappuccino. There's something about the free-spirited younger woman that fascinates her, but Madison refuses to be that weird older woman who hits on the barista – no matter how much she wants to.

Determined to move past her crush, Madison signs up for a lesbian dating site. To her shock, the woman she's matched with looks a little familiar...and despite their age gap, she and Camille are ninety-eight percent compatible.

On the surface, their lives couldn't be more different, but they're alike in all the ways that matter. Until a tragedy strikes, testing the strength of their new relationship.

"My Secret Crush" is book six in the "Friends to Lovers" contemporary lesbian romance series. Each book in the series is a steamy standalone featuring an LGBTQ couple making the leap from friends to lovers and looking for their "happily ever after".

*Be sure to check out a free preview of "The Divorcee's First Time" at the end of this book!*

# JOIN REBA BALE'S NEWSLETTER

Want a free book? Join my weekly newsletter and you'll receive a fun subscriber gift. I promise I will only email you when there are new releases, free books, or special sales you'll want to see.

Visit my newsletter sign-up page at https://books.rebab ale.com/lesbianromance to join today.

# DEDICATION

To everyone who loved someone from afar and was afraid to do something about it. Here's hoping you'll find a happily ever after. In the meantime, take a chance.

What have you got to lose?

# CAMILLE

**M**y eyes went to the clock. Seven twenty nine a.m. The door would be opening in five, four, three, two...

And there she was. My secret crush. Madison Phoenix. Billionaire CEO of Phoenix Software. The woman who didn't even know I was alive.

"Good morning Madison," I said pleasantly. "Triple grande nonfat cappuccino with a blueberry muffin?"

Madison came into Morning Jolt, the coffee shop where I worked, at precisely seven-thirty every morning, always ordering the exact same thing. Even after serving her coffee every single day for close to a year, she always seemed surprised that I remembered her order.

"Yes please," she said, her voice husky as if it was the first time she'd used it today. I couldn't help but wonder if that's what she sounded like when she first woke up. Our eyes met and held for several breaths before I looked away and keyed her order into the point of sale.

*Don't be a weirdo,* I told myself sternly. *She doesn't even know you exist outside of this coffee shop.*

"That'll be eight-ninety," I told her, the same as every day.

Madison scanned her payment with her phone, adding a five dollar tip. Same as every day. Madison was nothing if not predictable.

I grabbed the tongs and selected her muffin from the bakery case, sliding it into a paper bag emblazoned with the Morning Jolt logo. Handing the bag to Madison along with a napkin, I assured her, "Your cappuccino will be right up."

I studied her out of the corner of my eye while I made her drink. She wasn't very tall, maybe five four, but she carried herself with an unmistakable air of authority. Even if you didn't know she was one of the only female CEOs in Seattle's thriving software industry, if you ran into Madison on the street you'd definitely know she was in charge of *something*.

She was wearing her navy blue pantsuit today, the one that hugged her generous hips but was loose in the legs, tapering down too cuffed hems that fell just above her navy blue pumps. Yes, I had categorized every one of the prim outfits she wore to work. She had gone with a pristine white blouse beneath the jacket, the outline of her white bra faintly visible beneath the thin fabric. Her breasts were full, maybe a bit too big for her frame, but she kept them tightly cinched in what I imagined was an expensive bra.

Madison's dark brown hair was pulled back into a low ponytail, the style highlighting her sharp cheekbones and naturally tan skin. She looked like she had some Mediterranean blood, maybe Italian. Whatever her heritage, she was beautiful. And completely off limits.

She was wearing her blue framed glasses today, matching her suit. She seemed to have different frames to match every outfit. Behind the glasses, almond shaped brown eyes shone with intelligence.

Thanks to some internet stalking, I knew that she was thirty-five, ten years older than me. She'd started Phoenix in her dorm room at the University of Washington, developing a first-of-its-kind software that helped businesses and influencers to schedule social media posts in advance. By the time she'd gotten her MBA a few years later, Phoenix's software was one of the most popular options out there. The company had gone on to create several other super profitable products, making Madison and her early investors billionaires.

A therapist would probably have a field day with my obsession with Madison. I had a google alert on my phone for any mentions of her in the press, and I'd adjusted my work schedule so I could be here early and see her every weekday morning. It was totally lame, but the five minutes I spent with her each morning was the highlight of my day.

None of the articles I'd read had said anything about her personal life. She seemed to keep low-key outside of work. As far as I could tell, she didn't attend too many of those fancy charity events that rich people liked to attend, but when she did, she was usually accompanied by one of her staff.

I wished I could ask her out, but I didn't even know if she dated women. Not that it would matter. CEOs like Madison Phoenix did not date plain old ordinary baristas like me. Although I wasn't just a barista. Then again, my "little fantasy stories", as my sister called them, probably wouldn't be that impressive to someone like Madison either.

I created a heart out of foam, the design resting on the top of her cappuccino, then placed a lid over it, wondering if Madison had ever even noticed the foam hearts I left for her every day. Even if she had, she likely wouldn't think anything of it. A lot of baristas made designs in coffee. I wasn't that unique.

I walked back to the counter to give Madison her coffee.

"Here you go, Madison," I said with a friendly smile. "Have a great day. We'll see you tomorrow."

"You too," she said automatically.

I suppressed a sigh as she walked her shapely self out of the coffee shop. It wasn't healthy for me to have such a huge crush on a woman who didn't even know I was alive. Maybe I should join a dating app or something. That would help me get over this ridiculous crush. Several of my friends had met great women on a new dating site that was tailored to lesbians.

I resolved to sign up as soon as I got my break.

# MADISON

I blew out a breath as I exited the coffee shop. Just like every day, that cute barista was working the counter. And just like every day, I felt like a bumbling fool around her. She was so adorable. So sweet. So young. Younger than me, that's for sure.

Her name was Camille – that much I could tell from her name badge – but other than that I knew next to nothing about her. She was fresh-faced, maybe in her early twenties, with thick blonde hair that she wore in a messy bun, as if she was much too busy doing interesting things to have time to fuss with her hair.

Camille was a few inches taller than me, but then again, most people were. She was slim with toned arms and a smile that lit up the coffee shop. And those big brown eyes of hers...my God, I could just lose myself in them. Every time our eyes met, everything else seemed to fall away.

*You're being a pervert,* I chided myself. *You're practically old enough to be her mother.*

Well, that was an exaggeration, but we definitely had an age gap that was likely too far to bridge. Besides, what would a hot young girl like that want with a quickly approaching middle-aged woman like me? Assuming she even dated women.

She was friendly and flirty, but I shouldn't take it for more than what it was. It was part of her job, I needed to remember that. Just like the foam heart she drew on my coffee every day. I wasn't anything special to her.

I tried to put Camille out of my mind as I entered the building that housed Phoenix Software. I was proud of what I'd accomplished. I'd worked damn hard to make it in the uber competitive and predominantly male world of software development. I had a job I loved. More money than I could ever spend. A great townhouse in Seattle's fancy Belltown neighborhood. And a recently created foundation that was dedicated to addressing socioeconomic and educational inequities for women and girls.

And yet, I was lonely. I had friends, good friends even, but something was missing. A partner. Someone to snuggle on the couch with at night and wake up with in the morning. It had been a long time since I'd dated anyone. Way too long.

My best friend and employee Alice had been bugging me to try one of those matchmaking apps. There was one that was specifically for lesbians, and several people we knew had found love on the site. It felt pathetic to let an algorithm pick out a girlfriend for me, but then again, what was I going to do? Continue to obsess about the girl at the coffee shop?

I decided to sign up before I lost my nerve. I had the first hour of the day blocked off for administrative work, so I opened the site on my laptop and created an account. A few minutes later I had to admit that I was impressed.

No pictures were allowed on the site, just avatars you could create by inputting your physical characteristics. *True compatibility isn't physical,* the site explained. *We want you to get to know your potential match on the basis of who you are, not how you look.*

I input the key elements like height, weight, hairstyle, eye color, and skin tone and when I was done I had to admit my avatar bore more than just a passing resemblance to me.

Next was a lengthy questionnaire covering everything from what you wanted in a relationship, to how you dealt with conflict, to what your preferred leisure activities were. There were questions about physical attributes that you usually felt attracted to, as well as those you didn't, and a checklist of sexual preferences. It also asked you to be honest about the things that might be deal breakers or annoy potential partners, like being messy or compulsive flirting. I answered each question as honestly as I could and breathed a sigh of relief when I finally pressed "send".

*You don't have to go out with anyone*, I reminded myself. *Let's just see what happens.*

I must have said that part out loud, because I heard my best friend Alice call from the doorway, "See what happens about what?"

As usual, she looked impeccable in her pencil skirt, silk blouse, and high heels. Alice had found a partner last year, her best friend's little sister, Jewel. I'd been surprised that she was dating someone as young and carefree as Jewel, but I had to admit the relationship seemed to agree with Alice. My friend was happier and more relaxed than I'd seen her since we were in the MBA program together all those years ago.

"I finally signed up for that dating app everyone's talking about," I told her.

Alice clapped her hands together. "Yay! What made you finally decide to go through with it?"

I sagged back into my chair. "I keep fantasizing about the girl who works in the coffee shop."

"Which one?" Alice asked curiously.

"Camille." At her blank look I added, "She's about five seven, really toned arms, blonde hair she wears up in a messy bun."

"Oh yeah, she's adorable. Looks young, but God knows I'm not one to talk when I'm robbing the cradle with Jewel." Alice smiled as she thought of her younger girl-friend. "But then again, no one bats an eye when a guy dates someone ten or twenty years younger than him. You should ask her out."

I shook my head. "It's not just her age. I mean, what would we even have in common? I'm sure she gets hit on all the time, and she's flirting because it helps get tips."

"She flirts with you?" Alice asked.

At my nod she added, "I've never seen her be anything but professional when I've been in there. I've never seen her flirt with anyone."

"You probably don't notice people are flirting with you now that you have your own serious girlfriend," I teased. "How is Jewel anyway?"

"She's doing well. Working on a big fundraiser for the food bank, a big gala at the museum." Alice brightened. "You should bring Coffee Shop Girl!"

I shook my head. "No. Just no. But maybe I'll get a good match on the dating app, and I can bring them to the gala."

"Suit yourself," Alice said, getting up to leave. "I'll just say that this is the most interested I've seen you in a woman for a long time, which is definitely something you should think about Maddy. I've got to get to work, but I'll see you at the staff meeting this afternoon."

As Alice left, my computer dinged. I looked down to see a notification that the app had already matched me with seven different women, including one who was a ninety-eight percent match to me. I smiled. Maybe this would work out after all.

# CAMILLE

As soon as I got off work I checked my email. I'd signed up for that lesbian matchmaking site while I was on my break, but I didn't have enough time to see what kinds of matches would come up for me. I was dying to see if I'd matched with anyone.

I opened the app and to my surprise I'd already matched with eleven women. That was promising. The match at the top was ninety-eight percent compatible – almost a perfect match. I reviewed her profile.

She was a professional woman, ten years older than me, and liked hiking, watching movies, and visiting local breweries. So far so good. Like me she preferred to keep things neat but didn't do as well as she hoped. I continued to scan the information, noting all the ways we were similar.

I got down to the sexual preferences section and my eyes widened. She preferred to take a more submissive role in the bedroom and was interested in being tied up and light spanking, but nothing heavy. That lined up perfectly with my own preferences. I liked to be in control, but not in a "wear a collar and crawl behind me" way. I just liked to have a woman the tiniest bit at my mercy. I liked to order her around during sex and do a little power play. Not all the time, but it was definitely one of the things that got my motor running.

I glanced at the avatar that was connected to the profile. The program was designed to match on compatibility factors without allowing people to judge solely on looks. The avatar kind of reminded me of Madison. Even her physical description seemed to match. I shook my head at my silliness. Clearly I couldn't get Madison off my mind.

Well, whoever this woman was, according to the app we were almost a perfect match. Before I could change my mind, I sent her a message.

*Hey there TechGirl87,*

*I see that we're almost a perfect match. My question is, what do we need to do to get to 100%? Since we're both overachievers, I think we should definitely figure this out.*

*I've never done one of these sites before, so apologies for any gaffes. I'm not sure how to start a conversation so I'll just pretend that we met in a bar. First I'd offer to buy you a drink. If you ordered something frou-frou like a pina colada, I'd probably go to the bathroom and not come back. Kidding. Kind of.*

*What's your go-to bar drink order? Hope to hear from you soon.*

*Fantasy Writer*

A couple of hours later, the reply came. I'd turned on app notifications in my phone so I wouldn't have to keep checking it obsessively for a response.

*Hi Fantasy Writer,*

*Does your handle mean you're a writer? Do tell. I like a little fantasy myself, although I'm much more of a sci-fi girl. #GeekAtHeart*

*My go-to drink would really be a nice hoppy IPA, but I've found on dates people think that's a weird order, so I usually get a rum and coke instead. A good solid drink, but not as satisfying as an IPA.*

*I've also been pondering the mystery of our 2% incompatible score. I think the answer is dogs. You said you like them, I said I can take them or leave them. That's not a deal breaker for me, but I do need to be clear on one thing: I'll delete your profile if you tell me you have a snake. Or any type of reptile. Hoping you're not a fan of things that should remain in the jungle.*

*TechGirl87*

TechGirl87 and I spent the next week chatting through the app's text system. Every night and at random times throughout the day we'd exchange stories, information about ourselves, and information about what we were looking for in a relationship.

I was dying to meet her, dying to learn her real name, but we needed to be in contact for at least ten days before the app would let us share any personal details. We could of course just share that in our messages back and forth, but it was technically against the terms of service. Every time I opened the message app the system reminded me that sharing identifying information or making arrangements to meet were against the TOS and would result in a permanent ban from the site.

I decided to trust the process; there was a reason the site had these safeguards built in. Still, as much as I appreciated the safety features, it was hard to hold back. We were both eager to meet up and learn if the other person was as perfect as we seemed. I sure hoped so because I felt giddy every time my phone dinged with a message. And I was not a giddy person normally.

Meanwhile, I still saw Madison every morning at seven-thirty when she came in for her coffee. Something had seemed different about her this past week, although I couldn't really put my finger on it. *Probably because you don't know her, doofus,* I reminded myself. She just seemed...lighter somehow. A little more perky.

I just hoped that things worked out with TechGirl87. I'd been longing for a relationship, and even though we hadn't met in person, I felt really connected to her already. And maybe starting to date someone else would finally get my mind off of my ill-fated crush on Madison.

I was trying not to get my hopes up too soon, but my match and I seemed to have a lot in common. We both loved the same movies and most of the same activities, but we were divergent in enough ways that I knew if we got together we would still have our own lives. I'd been in a few relationships where the other person had immediately given up on anything other than me, and it was exhausting to feel fully responsible for someone else's free time. No one needed to be together twenty-four/seven, no matter how compatible they were. The fact that TechGirl87 was older and seemed to have her own life was promising.

After ten days of messaging back and forth, TechGirl87 and I were free to take things to the next level. We still hadn't shared our real names, but we decided to wait until we met in real life.

*That way if it's hate at first sight we can go back to being anonymous strangers who don't message each other several times a day,* she wrote.

We agreed to meet at a local park that had hiking trails. I think we were both imagining that if things were awkward at least we'd have something to do.

I sometimes picked up dog-sitting gigs, and I was taking care of a client's dog that morning. Since my client was meeting me at the dog park to pick up her dog, I asked TechGirl87 to meet me by the fenced in dog park.

I waited at the side of the dog park, alternating between watching the dog and waiting for TechGirl87. I'd just handed off the dog leash to my client when I heard a voice behind me say, "FantasyWriter? Is that you?"

Whoever she was talking to said, "No, sorry."

I said goodbye to my client and turned towards the familiar-sounding voice. My heart started racing as I realized who it was: Madison. My secret coffee shop crush.

# Madison

I looked around the park area, trying to figure out who FantasyWriter was and regretting our decision not to trade real names or at least share physical descriptions beyond our avatars.

"Madison?"

Someone called my name in a surprised voice. I turned to see Camille, the barista from the coffee shop.

"Oh. Hi. It's Camille, right?" I greeted her, as if her name wasn't tattooed on my soul.

Camille walked closer, stopping a couple of feet away from me.

"You're TechGirl87?" she asked.

My jaw dropped. "How did you know that?"

"Because I'm FantasyWriter."

"No you're not. You're the girl who makes my coffee at Morning Jolt."

She looked offended at my response. "And when I'm not working at the coffee shop I write fantasy books that I self-publish."

Damn it, I'd really put my foot in my mouth. "Oh. I'm sorry, I'm just...surprised."

"Disappointed?" she asked, looking young and vulnerable.

"No. Of course not," I replied, "It's just that you're not who I expected."

"Who were you expecting?" she asked. "We never ex-changed descriptions."

I was totally fucking this up. It was like my two fantasies had crashed into each other and I didn't quite know what to do.

"I just thought, uh, you'd be older," I explained. "I thought I'd put my lower age limit at twenty-five."

"I'm twenty-five."

I closed my eyes. She was a little older than I thought but at ten years younger than me she was definitely younger than the women I usually dated. Not that I'd done much dating lately.

"Shall we walk for a while?" she offered, breaking the silence. I appreciated her moving past the awkwardness.

We headed towards a trail, and I looked at her out the corner of my eye. She was wearing faded jeans that hugged her curvy ass, and a lightweight blue sweater. Her hair was down today, blonde waves going past her shoulders. She looked adorable.

I'd gone with jeans as well, although mine were dark washed. I'd paired them with a red knit shirt that accentuated my cleavage and complimented my skin tone.

"It's a weird coincidence, us getting matched," I said. "I mean, since we already kind of knew each other."

Camille nodded. "I guess it's fate."

We settled into a slow walk on the path, strolling beneath the tall trees and chatting easily once the initial awkwardness was over. The truth is I didn't like surprises. I was normally a planner who outlined every possibility. Structure and routine made me feel safe after an unstable childhood, and it also helped me be successful in my job. Camille being my dating app friend was unexpected, but not at all disappointing. In fact, it was serendipitous, and for once in my life, I decided just to go with the flow and see how things worked out.

When we came out on the other side of the trail I realized that an hour had passed so quickly I'd scarcely noticed. Camille was smart and funny and thoughtful, and it made for great conversation.

"Shall we get a drink?" I suggested, nodding towards the line of food carts set up between the park and the parking lot. "I didn't realize it would be so warm today. I'm parched."

I felt unaccountably pleased when Camille agreed. We both ordered a lemonade and after a brief scuffle over who was going to pay, my date bought our drinks, and we headed to a picnic table to enjoy our beverages.

Camille boosted herself up on the tabletop and I moved to sit next to her, enjoying her nearness. Free to think of her as a dating partner instead of someone who probably got tired of people hitting on her at work, my attraction to her ratcheted up dramatically. My attraction to coffee shop Camille had been purely physical – after all we'd never exchanged more than a few words here and there. My attraction to FantasyWriter was mental, based on our compatibility score and two weeks of messaging back and forth. But now that I knew they were the same person, I was enamored with the whole package.

"I have a confession to make."

Camille turned to look at me more directly. "Yeah?"

"I've kind of had a crush on you for a long time. I've actually been dying to ask you out, but I didn't want to make things weird. I'm sure customers hit on you all the time."

I didn't add that I'd masturbated to the thought of her so often I had to buy a new vibrator. Some things were better left private.

"I don't get hit on as much as you might think."

Camille leaned forward until our lips were only a couple of inches away. The air between us shimmered with heat.

"I'm glad to hear I'm not the only one with a crush," she whispered before closing the distance between us.

Her lips were soft as they pressed against mine gently. When I didn't pull back – my God, why would I? – she slid one hand behind my head and licked along the seam of my lips, demanding entrance. I opened my mouth with a sigh.

Our tongues tangled together, exploring. Camille's kiss was like a drug. I felt buzzy, the way you get when you're in that area between sober and drunk. I moaned and Camille deepened the kiss, taking over. The chatter that was always in my head decreased in volume as I let her take the lead. She might be younger than me, but it was clear she was the more dominant. And I liked to be the one who didn't need to do all the thinking or make all the decisions.

I wrapped my arms around her waist, trying to get closer as the kiss went on and on. When we finally pulled apart, we were both breathing heavily.

"We really shouldn't have waited so long to do that," Camille said as she moved back from me. My body immediately mourned her closeness.

"I agree," I responded. "But now that we know how good it is, when can we do it again?"

# CAMILLE

M y eyes went to the clock. Seven-thirty. Madison should be here...now. She rushed in looking the tiniest bit frazzled, and I wondered if she was regretting our time together yesterday.

I'd wanted nothing more to take her back to my place and ravish her. Or go to her place and ravish her, I wasn't picky about the location as long as ravishing was involved. But despite her bold words, I could see Madison's mind racing after that hot kiss. I knew instinctively that she was going to need some time to process what happened on the picnic table. I didn't know her very well yet, but it was clear she was a thinker. A processor. A planner. So, after we drank our lemonades, I'd walked her back to her car and left her with a hug, then spent the entire night thinking about her.

"Good morning Madison," I said in my best customer service voice.

Madison gave me a grateful smile, making me wonder if she thought I was going to do something weird to embarrass her. "Hi."

"You want your usual?"

"Yes please. Thanks Camille."

A couple of customers lined up behind her as I bagged up her muffin and made her cappuccino. As usual, I made a heart in the foam for her. What wasn't usual was the way I deliberately rubbed my hand against hers as I handed her the coffee. Madison leaned close and lowered her voice to a whisper.

"Can I call you tonight?"

We'd exchanged phone numbers at the park yesterday, so we didn't have to keep messaging through the dating app. I'd hesitated about texting her though, wanting to give her time.

I nodded, my heart lightening as I realized that Madison wasn't going to pull away from whatever was happening between us. But then I wondered if she just wanted to call me to break it off. Damn it, I hated feeling unsure like this. It wasn't like me.

Madison called a few minutes after five. I was working on my latest novel when the phone rang, so I saved my file before I answered. I wasn't taking the book world by storm, but my books had gotten enough of a following that I was paying my rent with the royalties.

"Hey Camille, it's Madison. How was your day?"

"Good. And yours?"

Madison hesitated. "It was okay, well not really, but anyway, I was wondering, I mean I know this is very last minute, but are you free for dinner?"

I suppressed a smile at her cute babbling. I was a little surprised by her offer. I'd wondered if after she processed that kiss in the park she would decide to call things off. I was glad she wanted to see me again. But something felt a little off in her voice. I couldn't decide what it was.

"Sure, where were you thinking?"

When she paused I asked, "Are you okay?"

"Um. Yeah. I just had a bit of a rough day. Sorry. Now that I'm thinking about this, I might not be the best company tonight."

I had the sense that her desire to see me was warring with her need to be perfect. Maybe she just needed a friend tonight.

"How about if we just order some food and watch a movie at your place?" I asked. "Then we can just hang out, no pressure."

Madison's voice sounded relieved. "That sounds perfect, actually."

"Okay, how about you text me your address and I'll come over with food."

"I can order --."

I interrupted her. "Text me your address and I'll bring food."

"Okay. I should be home by six thirty."

"See you then."

I took a quick shower, then checked my phone. Madison's house wasn't too far from my favorite Italian place. Perfect. I called in an order then headed out to the car. By the time I got to the restaurant, our order was ready. Fifteen minutes later I was on Madison's porch with a giant bag of carby goodness.

"Oh. Camille. Hi."

Madison was coming up the stairs behind me, still wearing the business clothes she'd had on this morning.

I held up the bag. "I hope you're not gluten free."

It felt like half the population of Seattle was gluten free. Or dairy free. Or nightshade free. Or vegan. Or some combination of those things.

She fake shuddered. "Oh God. No. I love my gluten."

"I knew I liked you."

She moved past me to open the door. "The kitchen is through there," she said, pointing. "If you don't mind, I'm going to change my clothes."

"Go right ahead."

I walked through her townhouse. It was nice. Understated. Everything was clearly expensive, but not ostentatiously so. I liked it, although it could use some color. Almost everything was white.

I made my way to the kitchen, opening cabinets and drawers until I found plates and utensils. I stacked them on the counter and unpacked the food. The scent of garlic filled the air, making my stomach rumble and reminding me that I hadn't eaten lunch.

"Oh my God, that smells incredible," Madison said happily as she came into the kitchen wearing stretchy yoga pants and a tank top with an unzipped hoodie, her hair released from its signature ponytail. She looked younger and softer like this. I liked it.

"I wasn't sure what you liked," I said, "so I got a few things." I pointed at the containers. "Lasagna. Fettuccini alfredo. Ravioli. Salad. Oh, and garlic bread."

"I think I love you," she joked, then her eyes widened. "Oh, I mean..."

I held up a hand to stop her sputtering. She was so cute when she was flustered, it was a big change from her usual in-control CEO persona.

"It's good. I know what you mean. Shall we eat?"

We filled our plates and took our food to the living room. I looked through her Netflix queue while Madison got us drinks. I put on something mindless, one of the newer comic book superhero movies that had a female protagonist and settled on the couch. Madison returned, handing me a bottle of a locally brewed beer, and settling on the opposite end of the couch.

"Why are you so far away?" I asked.

She quickly scooched closer, and I hid a smile at how she responded to me. We tucked into our food and spent the next hour watching the movie. Pausing midway, I went to the bathroom while Madison cleared the plates and brought us each another beer.

"I feel so much better," she sighed as she plopped back onto the couch. Her eyes were still a bit troubled though.

"Do you want to talk about it?" I asked, turning to face her.

Madison's face turned sad, and she shook her head, then started talking. "It's nothing, just a hard day at work."

I grabbed her hand, ignoring the way my skin tingled from her touch. "I don't want to force you to talk Madison, but sometimes it's nice to have someone on the outside to share with."

She gave me a long look. "I fired someone today. Then I had them arrested."

# MADISON

I searched Camille's face, looking for signs of judgement, and finding none, continued my story.

"There's this guy I went to college with. A nice guy. Well, I thought he was a nice guy," I began. "When I hired him, I brought him on as my numbers guy, the Chief Financial Officer. But lately some weird things have been happening. More discrepancies than usual on financial reports. Things not adding up the way they used to. I'm not a finance person, but I was seeing a pattern in the numbers that didn't make sense."

Camille nodded but didn't speak, only reaching out to grab my hand. The press of her soft fingers around mine was incredibly comforting.

"I'd asked Mark – the CFO – to look into it and he'd assured me that it was nothing. Just normal anomalies. But he's been acting different the last year too, more non-communicative, kind of snippy. Not the Mark I've known all these years. I'd chalked it up to his wife leaving him last year, but I was starting to wonder if there was more there. So, I secretly brought in a forensic auditor and asked them to review our books. And..."

I paused, the pain of Mark's betrayal creating a lump in my throat.

"He was embezzling?" Camille guessed.

I nodded. "Yeah. I had them check twice. I told myself it wasn't him, it had to be someone else on the team, but...it was him. We were able to trace the missing money to his personal accounts. I confronted him with my HR director and the police this morning. He changed his story a few times. First he denied it. Then he said his mother was sick and he needed money to help her, then it was he'd gotten behind on bills, all of which is ridiculous. He makes a shit ton of money. Then he totally broke down and admitted he's been gambling. He's been stealing money to cover his bad bets. Hundreds of thousands of dollars. I had him arrested."

Camille studied me for a long moment. "Of course you had him arrested. He not only betrayed you, but he also broke the law."

Her matter-of-fact response helped me feel slightly better. "I just wish --."

She held up her hand. "He's responsible for his actions. Not you. I get that he probably has an addiction, but he's still the person who made the decision to place that first bet. To steal that first dollar, and every one after that. He made those choices, not you."

"I just feel like I should've done something. Asked him why he was acting so weird. Paid attention to the red flags I've been seeing for the last year."

She squeezed my fingers. "You can only control yourself Madison. You can't control other people, and you really can't help them make better decisions if they're dead set on doing the opposite."

I nodded. She was right, I knew she was. But learning that my friend wasn't who I thought he was still hit me like a punch to the gut.

"Well, thanks for listening."

I leaned forward, intending to give her a hug, but somehow we wound up kissing instead. Our lips met and we moved closer as Camille slid her tongue against mine, exploring. She took control immediately.

I'd been surprised last time we kissed at how she automatically took the lead. It had never been like this with any of the other women I'd been with, or even the men. I was always the one moving things along, kind of like in my career. A few times I'd suggested that partners tie me up or at least take control, but they'd always acted like I was being weird. I didn't want to be in charge of everything all the time, it was exhausting. With Camille it felt nice to take a backseat, to let someone else lead the way.

Camille's lips were soft but firm, and I could taste the garlic on her breath, making me realize it was likely the same for her. I pulled away.

"What's the matter?" she asked, her brow crinkling. "Am I moving too fast?"

"My breath...the garlic..."

Camille rolled her eyes, then placed one hand on each of my shoulders. "I want you Madison. I don't care about your breath. I think you need to learn to get out of your head a bit."

"What do you mean?"

She stood up. "Lay on your back."

Her voice sounded kind of bossy. I liked it.

I moved to lay on the couch, looking up at her curiously.

"Put your hands over your head," she ordered. "Grab onto the armrest and don't let go."

I reached overhead, my hands landing on the cushioned arm rest. Camille walked to the other end of the couch, pulling my yoga pants down my legs as she went. My shirt had ridden up, exposing the soft rolls of my tummy, and my hands moved down automatically to cover the area from her gaze.

Camille landed a sharp slap on my right thigh. "What did I tell you about your hands? Do I need to tie you up?"

A rush of arousal flooded my core so quickly that I knew my panties were going to be completely soaked. I raised my hands back to the arm rest obediently.

"Good girl."

Another rush of arousal. Hmm. Apparently I liked being praised?

Camille dropped to her knees next to the couch, lifting one hand to cup my mound. Her eyes flew to mine, a satisfied smirk twisting her lips.

"Well. Aren't you soaking wet?"

I felt my cheeks flame.

"Is this all for me?"

When I didn't answer, she slapped her hand against my cloth-covered pussy. "Answer me."

It stung and yet, it felt incredible.

"Yes," I whined. "It's for you."

Grabbing the elastic waist of my satin panties, Camille slid them off, tossing them on the floor behind her. She stared at my pussy for a long moment, making me rub my thighs together.

"Oh no," she chided. "You don't hide yourself from me. Open up."

I slid my thighs apart to each side of the cushions, and Camille slid one finger through my folds, gathering up some of my wetness before bringing the finger to her mouth. She stared at me while she sucked my essence off her fingers. I damn near came on the spot.

Camille slid onto the bottom of the long couch, wriggling her way up between my thighs. I moved one leg onto the back of the couch to make space, and she pulled the other one up over her shoulder. She looked up at me from her spot between my legs.

"If you're not ready for this, if you feel uncomfortable or you want to stop, tell me now."

"I don't want to stop."

She gave me another smile.

"Remember, keep your arms up or no orgasm for you."

My entire body lit up with excitement. "Got it."

I watched as Camille lowered her head, her face disappearing into my center. She licked up and down several times, exploring my pussy with her tongue. It felt incredible. Every time she reached my apex I gripped the armrest, desperate to slide my fingers into her hair and direct her to where I needed her most.

"Camille. I need..."

"I know what you need, you greedy girl. Be good and you'll get what you want."

She chuckled as another flood of moisture made its way down my core.

"You like being called a good girl?" she asked.

I nodded. She pinched my hip, the sting briefly intense.

"I didn't hear you."

I thrilled at her dominance. It was everything I never knew I needed. I'd never been this turned on in my entire life.

"Yes," I gasped. "I like it."

She nodded then returned to licking my pussy. Her tongue swirled around and around my clit, teasing me but never getting where I needed her touch the most. I was a mess beneath her, whining and shaking, begging her to bring me some relief.

"Please, Camille. Please."

"You want to come?" she asked darkly.

"Yes," I gasped.

"Ask me nicely."

There was no reason why I liked this, but damned if I didn't.

"Please Camille, will you let me come now?"

She nodded against my legs. "Since you asked nicely I won't make you beg. This time."

She shoved one finger deep into my channel, pumping roughly at the same time as she finally – finally – sucked my clit into her mouth. The instant her lips closed around the engorged bundle of nerves, biting down softly, I came with a long wail.

"Oh my God!"

I was flying, my body no longer tethered to the Earth as a flood of sensations hit me at once. The feeling of releasing control. The finger in my channel. The soft press of teeth against my clit. And the tsunami of an orgasm that crashed its way down my body and back again, leaving me breathless and drained.

When I stopped shaking, Camille moved up the couch, her knees on either side of my shoulders.

"I'm going to sit on your face and you're going to make me come," she told me. "And you're going to do it without moving your hands, okay?"

I nodded, then hastened to speak. "Yes."

# CAMILLE

I scooted a little higher on the couch so I could straddle Madison's head, then lowered myself down to sit on her face. I loved this position, it was dirty and dominant and a great way to get myself off.

The instant I got close enough, Madison began dutifully licking up and down my seam. I shivered with excitement. After all these months, maybe over a year, of fantasizing about Madison eating me out, I was ready to come almost immediately.

Determined to stretch this out a bit, I braced one hand on the back of the couch and the other one in her hair, directing her motions. Her hands were still clutching the side of the couch, her arms now trapped in place between my knees. I could feel how much she was dying to touch me, her hands twitching against the fabric as her body strained closer to me.

Madison's clever tongue slid into my channel, and she fucked me as deep as she could go. It felt incredible. I ground myself shamelessly against her face, forcing her to go deeper. I was close, so close, but I lifted up slightly to make sure she could breathe. No sense smothering her the first time around, although I did wonder if she was open to some breath play in the future.

While I was pondering that question, Madison lifted her head slightly, her hair pulling tight against my fingers, and wrapped her lips around my clit. It was so swollen it was painful, but I relaxed back down, reveling in the feeling of her swirling her tongue around the little nub. When she added suction, sucking me hard, that was it for me. I came with a shout.

"Fuck!"

I rolled my hips wildly against her face, simultaneously wanting more and wanting to pull back, but she kept a good hold on my clit until the shudders slowed and I came down from the powerful orgasm. It was incredible, even better than I'd imagined. And God knows I'd imagined it a million times.

Mindless of my weight on her face, I slid off her and onto the floor, landing on my knees next to the couch. I rested my head on her chest, just above her tits, panting and realizing ruefully that we were both still fully dressed from the waist up.

Oh well, we had time. Because now that I'd had Madison, there was no way I'd ever let her go.

"Do you want to stay over?" Madison's sweet voice brought me out of my thoughts. I looked up and smirked as I saw she still had her hands over her head.

"You can relax your hands."

She sprung up to seated, throwing her leg over my head so that I was kneeling on the floor between her legs. She squeezed her knees against my waist and leaned forward to capture my lips with hers. The kiss was sweet and almost chaste, yet perfect.

We pulled away and stared at each other for a long moment.

"I'd love to sleep over," I said, answering her earlier question.

She stood up, taking my hand. "Let's go to bed."

I followed her to her bedroom, taking in the large four-postered bed pushed against one wall. The room was very...white. White walls, white curtains, white furniture, white bedding.

"You like white, huh?"

Madison looked around in confusion. "I guess."

"I can't wait to tie you to this bed," I told her.

Madison smiled shyly. "I've never been tied up before, but I've fantasized about it a lot. I think I'll like it."

"Oh, you'll like it," I said confidently. "Now how about you take off your shirt so I can suck your tits?"

Her eyes darkened at my words. "I had no idea you were such a dirty talker," she said, as she dropped her hoodie and pulled her tank top over her head, leaving her wearing only a white satin bra.

She reached behind her to unclasp it, adding, "But I kind of like it."

I took off my own shirt and bra, and once we were both naked, we fell on the bed, kissing and touching each other like it was the first time either of us had seen a naked woman. It might not have been the first time for either of us, but for me, it was the first time I'd been naked with someone I loved. Someone who meant more than a quick fuck or a short-term relationship.

My eyes widened as I realized it was true. I'd thought what I felt for Madison was just a crush, and I guess it probably was, but after even a short time together dating, I knew it was more than that. Maybe it was crazy, or maybe the dating app's algorithms were correct, because I was already head over heels for Madison. I just hoped she would feel the same, if not now, then soon.

We fell into a pattern over the next month. Every morning I'd wake up wrapped around Madison, slipping quietly out of bed to make my way to the coffee shop for my five a. m. shift. Just like she'd been doing for over a year, Madison would come into the shop promptly at seven-thirty, and I'd make her a cappuccino and give her a muffin. She was always strictly professional with me at my work, which I appreciated, with never more than a secret smile or a slight brush of the hands between us as I passed her breakfast to her.

After my shift I'd go home and write, then Madison would text me when she was leaving work and we'd either meet for dinner some place or I'd head over to her house. Madison's place wasn't too ostentatious, but still the bathroom in her house was the size of my entire one-bedroom apartment, so it was much more comfortable to hang out there.

We would spend the night talking or watching movies or reading. Sometimes I would work on one of my books while Madison did some work, and then we'd spend the night together.

Our lovemaking was creative and energetic, and we couldn't get enough of each other. Madison might not have been tied up before she met me, but she took to it like a natural. It was clear that Madison's past lovers, both male and female, hadn't been the most creative, and I was happy to rectify that. I loved to try new things, learn what my partner liked, learn what gave us both the most pleasure.

Madison was close-mouthed about her feelings for me, but I knew for sure things were heading in the right direction when she suggested that we go on a double date with her best friend Alice and Alice's girlfriend Jewel. Like us, they were a couple with an age gap.

"Alice is my sister's best friend," Jewel explained over dinner. "We both thought my sister would freak out when we got together, but she took the news better than we expected."

"Once she realized you were a lesbian," Alice reminded her.

Turning to us, she added, "Jewel only came out to her family recently."

"Really?" I asked. "Why?"

"I was overseas in the Peace Corps, it just didn't really come up."

Alice rolled her eyes and fake coughed, "*Chicken shit.*"

Jewel laughed and nudged her with an elbow. "It all worked out fine, didn't it?"

"Will I see you at the gala?" Jewel asked as we finished dinner.

"Gala?" I looked between her and Madison, noting that my girlfriend looked a little bit uncomfortable. That's right, I was calling her my girlfriend already, even though we hadn't had "the talk" yet.

"I do community engagement at the food bank," Jewel told me. "We have our annual gala in a couple of weeks. It's our biggest fundraiser of the year. Black tie, totally fancy. Usually most of Seattle's elite are there."

When Madison remained silent, I demurred. "Um, we'll see."

Alice and Jewel gave us curious looks but didn't press the issue. Alice changed the subject, and the rest of the night passed quickly.

As we were walking out of the restaurant, Jewel leaned in to give me a hug. "Even if you don't come to the gala, I hope to see you again soon."

I waited until we got to the car before I turned to Madison. "Am I not your date for the gala?"

# MADISON

I could feel Camille's eyes on me the whole walk to the car.

"Am I not your date for the gala?" she asked as soon as we slid into our seats.

I looked at her, trying to gauge her mood from her expression. She looked curious, and maybe a little hurt. When I didn't answer, she crossed her arms over her body.

"It's okay," she said, her voice cold. "You're not obligated to invite me. I thought we were a couple now, what with us meeting each other's friends and all. I'm sorry if I made assumptions."

"You're not making assumptions." I rushed to reassure her. "We are. A couple I mean. I thought that was assumed but just to be clear, I want us to be a couple Camille. An exclusive couple."

"So, what is it then?" she asked. "Why wouldn't you invite me to something that's clearly important to you and your friends? Are you embarrassed of me or something? Afraid that I'll eat with my fingers or pick my nose in front of your fancy society friends?"

My heart pinched. "No, no it's not that at all. And I don't really have any fancy society friends. All of my friends are people I knew before I was wealthy. Except for you. You're the first new friend I've made in years."

"Then why don't you want me there?"

Camille raised her eyebrows, staring at me while I formulated my answer. I was surprised by her reaction. There was nothing in my experience with Camille so far that led me to believe that she'd ever have even the remotest interest in attending a black tie event. I'd never even seen her in anything besides jeans and shorts. But it was clear she was hurt, so I needed to tell her the truth.

"I've never taken a woman to an event before."

She frowned. "What do you mean? You were planning to bring a guy? I didn't realize you were bi."

"I'm not."

"Are you ashamed of being a lesbian?" she asked, her voice shocked. "Worried about what people would say about that?"

"No, of course not. I'm perfectly comfortable with who I am. It's just, well, I've seen so many of my colleagues have their privacy invaded after they became wealthy. Who they're dating, what their partner is wearing, it all becomes a topic for gossip or worse yet, something posted on social media. One of my vice-presidents was dating a plus size woman, and she was eviscerated online, such hateful comments, that the girl broke up with him because she couldn't take the scrutiny. I just never wanted to put anyone through that – male or female."

She seemed to consider my words.

"Are you saying that you didn't invite me because you thought I couldn't handle a little cyber bullying?"

"Honestly since I never take anyone to these events, it didn't even cross my mind to ask you. I usually go solo to these things."

She rolled her eyes, but her shoulders relaxed. I breathed a sigh of relief.

"Well guess what? You have a date for your fancy event whether you like it or not. And I have the perfect outfit for it too."

Two weeks later I had to agree: Camille had the perfect outfit.

I pulled up in front of her apartment and stepped out of the back door of the limo before the driver could come around. My breath caught in my throat.

Camille was wearing a skintight blue dress that managed to be both sexy and respectable. It was an off-the-shoulder design, keeping her creamy white shoulders bare but leaving strips of fabric around the top of her toned arms. The bodice ran straight across, hugging her gorgeous breasts. A belt made of matching fabric was snug against her waist, leading down to an A-line skirt that flared out just above her knees. She'd paired the outfit with matching shoes that added a good three inches to her height and had twisted her blonde hair back into a sophisticated twist that left several artful tendrils of blonde hair framing her face.

I'd never seen Camille wear make-up before, but tonight she'd given herself a smoky eye, a couple of layers of mascara, and deep red lips. She looked stunning. I felt breathless, thinking that I wanted nothing more than to pull her back into her apartment and mess her up again.

"You brought a limo?" she called, her tone teasing. "Isn't that overkill?"

"Nothing but the best for my girlfriend."

The driver came around and held the door open politely, waiting for us to get in. "Shall we?"

Camille's sharp eyes took in my pale pink dress, just a few shades pinker than white. It had cap sleeves and a sweetheart neckline that accentuated my boobs, the skirt falling down half the distance between my knees and ankles. I was wearing black ankle boots with a chunky heel, giving a slightly edgy look to the otherwise conservative dress. I'd pulled my hair back in a half bun, leaving the bottom half to cascade down my back.

She walked closer, her eyes glowing, and pressed a chaste kiss on my lips. "You look fabulous," she whispered. "I'll spend the entire night thinking about getting you out of that dress and fucking you with those shoes on."

I felt my face flush as I glanced at the driver, but if he'd heard her I couldn't tell by his impassive face.

I slid into the limo behind her and after closing the door, the driver headed towards the art museum where the event would be held. Camille and I looked straight ahead, each lost in thought as the driver navigated his way through the Seattle traffic.

Flashbulbs started going off the moment the driver opened the door to let me out, and I looked back to see Camille looking a bit like a deer in the headlights. I reached my hand in.

"Come on. They have no idea whether we're anyone famous or not so they're getting ready. Just look straight ahead and keep moving. They'll lose interest when they realize we're not famous."

We walked hand in hand up the ostentatious red carpet, checking in with the security team at the front entrance to confirm our invitation. Once inside we made the rounds, saying hello to people I knew, Camille clutching my hand the entire way. She was nothing but cool and confident, but I could tell she felt a bit out of her league here.

"You won't mess anything up," I whispered in her ear.

"What?"

"You seem worried. Don't be. You've got this."

Her expression smoothed, telling me I was right. It was an interesting turn of events. Despite our age difference, generally it was Camille who was the confident one in our relationship, the one who was reassuring me. I loved that, just this once, I got to be the one who did the reassuring.

We were seated at a large table with three other couples who were good friends of Jewel and Alice, including a famous rock star named Lila and her assistant and girlfriend Christine, our mutual friend Miranda and her partner Elizabeth, and a new couple to the group, Elana and Toya. I knew that they all hung out in a big, loosely knit group that also included a few other couples. I'd hung out with the group occasionally when I wasn't working, but I wasn't particularly close to anyone here besides Alice. And Camille, of course.

After dinner and the requisite speeches asking for money, the rest of the night passed quickly. We all talked and danced and laughed and got a little tipsy, making me grateful that I'd had the foresight to reserve the limo for me and Camille, so we didn't need to worry about driving or waiting around for an Uber.

When we got home, Camille slid my dress off my body, then removed my bra and panties, leaving me standing just in my boots. She leaned me over the side of the bed and tied my hands behind me with a scarf.

"Did you have fun, baby?" she asked as I heard the telltale sound of a vibrator turning on.

"Yeah."

Camille stroked me a few times with her hand before slipping the bullet vibrator into my channel. It started off slow but sped up as she hit the remote control. I pressed my face into the comforter, biting back a moan as the vibrations ramped up.

"Did you wear these boots to drive me crazy?" she asked.

"Maybe..."

My words were cut off as Camille's palm came down on my ass, giving me a sharp slap. I whined.

"You liked that?"

"You know I do."

Her hand came down again, and I could feel the heat traveling from my ass cheek right to my core as she spanked me a few times more.

"Your cheeks are pink," she said with satisfaction. "Just beautiful."

Then she reached around and teased my clit with her fingers until I came with a scream that I was pretty sure the neighbors heard. My orgasm slammed through me until I lay boneless on the bed, panting.

Camille helped me move up on the bed, removing the vibrator and the boots, and cuddling me in her arms.

"We should take care of you," I protested weakly, even though my eyelids were so heavy I could scarcely stay awake.

Camille kissed the top of my head. "You can eat me out for breakfast," she promised. "Sleep now."

# CAMILLE

Seven thirty a.m. Time for my girlfriend to come for coffee. Madison and I had been dating for four months now, and I'd learned that her need for schedules and routine had come from growing up in a chaotic home.

A couple of weeks ago I'd met her mother, a self-absorbed woman who gave 'flighty' a bad name, and her father, an inattentive misogynist who thought women should stay in the kitchen and marry men not, as he put it, 'cavort around with other gals'. I wasn't clear why they were still married other than they were equally horrible but meeting her parents had definitely filled in some missing pieces for me about Madison.

My parents were dead, but I introduced Madison to my twin sister Cassie and her husband and gotten the "Cassie seal of approval" as my sister called it. Madison was the same age as my brother-in-law Jake, reminding me that people didn't bat an eye when the guy was ten years older than a woman. It was such a double standard. But if anyone in our lives thought our age gap was a problem, they never mentioned it to either of us, which I appreciated.

I knew it sometimes bothered Madison, but I didn't care at all about the difference in our ages. We were similar enough in other ways.

Seven thirty came and went and I grew concerned. It wasn't like Madison to be late. Ever. She'd been fine when I left this morning. Well, sleeping but fine. At eight o'clock I texted her to see if she was okay, but I didn't receive a response. Nothing when I tried again at eight thirty. I couldn't imagine what would have happened to make Madison break her routine.

I was starting to really freak out when Alice called me just after nine o'clock.

"Hi Camille, I'm so sorry to bother you when you're at work, but have you seen Madison today?" Alice's voice sounded worried.

I shook my head even though she couldn't see me.

"No, she was sleeping when I left for work, but she never showed up for her seven thirty coffee stop," I explained. "It's not like her to break her routine."

"She's not at work either," Alice told me. "I'm really worried. She's not answering her work or personal phones. I'm thinking I should go to her house and check on her."

"I'll meet you there."

After telling my boss that I had a personal emergency, I grabbed an Uber over to Madison's house. It was faster than going back to my apartment for my car. Alice was pulling up at the same time as me.

We knocked on the door, but Madison didn't answer. I didn't have a key, which now that I thought of it was kind of weird given all the time I spent here, but fortunately Alice had one. She dug it out of her purse and opened the door for us.

We found Madison on the couch, dressed for work but with tears running down her face. I rushed over, Alice hot on my heels.

"Madison, what happened?"

She blinked at me with bleak eyes, a sob the only sound coming out of her mouth. What the fuck?

"Madison," Alice said sharply.

My girlfriend looked at her like she'd never seen her friend before. I put my arm around Madison and squeezed her tight, but she stayed stiff in my arms.

"Madison. What. Happened?" I asked again. She looked between Alice and me and started sobbing.

"It's Mark. He's...dead...killed...self."

I looked at Alice in confusion, hoping she knew who Mark was, because I certainly didn't.

"Mark killed himself?" Alice looked horrified, her eyes filling with tears. "I thought they watched people in jail for stuff like that. That stupid asshole."

The pieces clicked into place. "Is Mark the guy who embezzled from your company?"

Madison nodded. "I had him arrested," she wailed. "And now he killed himself."

"You had to do it Madison," Alice reminded her. "He stole from the company, and he broke the law."

"I should have gotten him help," she sobbed. "This is all my fault. He's dead because of me."

"It's not your fault Madison," I said firmly. "I know it feels that way right now, but Mark is responsible for his decisions, not you. And you can't help someone who doesn't want help."

She shook her head. "You don't understand. No one can understand what this feels like. Please, I need you both to leave. I just want to be alone."

"Madison, you shouldn't be alone right now," Alice said. "We can get through this together."

Madison pulled away from me, leaping off the couch. "Out!" she screamed shrilly. "Both of you. I need you to go away. Go. Now!"

Alice and I exchanged a look, both of us wondering if it was better to stay or obey Madison's wishes and leave her in this state.

"I can come back later, after work," I offered. "I'll bring lunch."

"No," she yelled. "Please. Both of you, leave now. I just want to be alone. Go. And don't come back."

She placed a shaky hand on my back, and another on Alice's arm, damn near shoving us out the door.

"Madison," I tried again, but she just slammed the door in our faces, leaving me wondering what the hell had just happened.

# Madison

I t had been three days since I got the news about Mark. Three days of Alice and Camille calling, texting, showing up on the doorstep, and me ignoring them both. I felt worse than I'd felt in my entire life, and time was not making the pain any better. It was Friday and I was looking forward to a weekend of peace and quiet. Hopefully.

I knew I needed to get my ass back to work, but I couldn't quite focus yet. I was overwhelmed with guilt about what happened to Mark. I'd learned that his lawyer had been encouraging him to take a plea bargain, telling him that there was an ironclad case against him, leaving almost zero chance that he'd be acquitted. The lawyer had warned that Mark was looking at a lengthy prison sentence, and apparently that had been the thing that had put him right over the edge. He'd used his bed sheets to hang himself. Even though I obviously hadn't seen him, every time I closed my eyes I could see Mark hanging there in his cell, lifeless.

My phone buzzed with another text from Camille. I knew she was trying to be supportive, but suddenly I just couldn't do this anymore. My friend was dead because of me, and I was too overwhelmed to do anything but wallow in misery.

**Camille:** *How are you doing? Do you need anything? Dinner maybe?*

**Madison:** *I'm sorry, but I've been giving it a lot of thought, and this thing just between us just isn't going to work out.*

**Camille:** *You're breaking up with me?!?!*

**Madison:** *Yes.*

**Camille:** *You're breaking up with me -- over text -- because someone who stole from you killed themselves? I can't believe you're doing this. I don't mean to be insensitive, but I don't see*

> *the connection here. I thought things were good between us.*

She was right, things *had* been good between us. And that was what was bothering me the most. While we were having fun, Mark – a man who I'd once considered a close friend -- had been rotting away in a jail cell because I'd never noticed how much he needed help. Mark had killed himself while I was going to fancy galas with a younger woman, too wrapped up in my new relationship to even think about him. I didn't deserve to be happy when my friend was dead. What if I failed Camille like I'd failed Mark?

> **Madison:** *I had fun with you and you're a great girl. I wish you all the best. Please don't contact me again.*

> **Camille:** *You wish me all the best? What the actual fuck? Fine, I won't contact you again. For the record, I thought you were the woman I was going to spend the rest of my life with. You have no idea how glad I am to find out who and what you really are before we made a commitment. Have a nice life. Not.*

I re-read her text about a thousand times as the tears fell. I knew I'd been an asshole to Camille – something she didn't deserve since God knows she'd never been anything but supportive and loving to me – but I just couldn't see my way out of it. The grief was so all-consuming it was like a living thing that was taking over my life.

On Monday I dragged my sorry ass into work for the first time in nearly a week. I'd skipped my favorite coffee shop, given that I needed to avoid Camille like the plague now, and settled for a disappointing cappuccino from one of the national chain stores. Apparently crappy coffee was part of my self-imposed penance. They didn't even do the foam heart that Camille always did for me. God, I missed her so much, and not just for her coffee.

Alice swooped in the minute I got to the office, but I waved her off with a frown. "Not now Alice, I need to catch up."

I waved to my administrative assistant. "I need updates please."

I got through the entire week avoiding my friends. I threw myself into my work, putting in long hours not only to catch up on what I missed but also to keep my mind off of everything. As my life returned to a sense of normalcy, my perspective started to return as well.

Things had looked much bleaker when I was alone in my house crying on the couch. Back in the world of the people who worked and showered and wore pants, the guilt I felt about my former friend's death gradually lessoned. And with that, I regained some of my perspective.

When Alice barged into my office at the end of the day Friday with our social worker friend Miranda, I knew my grace period with her was up. I'd been dodging her all week other than when we had to interact for work. I was only surprised she'd let me get away with it for so long.

"We need to talk."

Alice closed the door and gave me a firm look while Miranda gave me a look that was a bit more empathetic. "We've been worried about you Madison."

I waved them both towards the seating area at one end of the office. They each took a chair, leaving me to sit on the small loveseat like I was a psych patient being tag-teamed by a team of therapists. And maybe that's what I needed.

"Before you ask, I'm fine. Or getting there." I looked between my friends. "I know you've been worried, but I needed some time to process everything."

"What happened with Mark wasn't your fault," Miranda said softly. "I know his actions hurt you, but people make their own choices."

"I know. I just needed some time. I needed to grieve in my own way."

Alice, the bad cop in this scenario, sent me a stern look.

"You've had enough time to wallow Madison. You can't just ignore your responsibilities. Mark was my friend too you know, and I'm sad as hell that he decided to go out that way. But that was his choice, everything that happened was his choice, and there's nothing that you or I or anyone else could've done. You know we can't save people who don't want saving."

I nodded. "Yeah."

"And what the hell happened with Camille?" Alice continued, clearly on a roll now. "She said you broke up with her. Via text message."

For the first time, Miranda sent me a disapproving look. "You broke up with her in a text? That woman is the best thing that ever happened to you. You've seemed so much happier since you two started dating."

I collapsed back on the couch, knowing I looked as miserable as I felt.

"I know. I made a terrible mistake."

"Well thank Christ you figured that one out," Alice muttered.

I frowned. "I needed some time, and she was just...there. Calling and texting and coming over to check on me, it was all too much."

"That evil bitch! How dare she try to support you in your time of need!"

Alice's sarcasm wasn't lost on me. "Yeah, yeah, but I wasn't in my right mind. I just kept thinking she would be better off without me, without someone who can't save their friend."

"Oh for fuck's sake, I can't believe --."

Miranda put her hand on Alice's arm to interrupt her rant, then leaned forward to look me in the eye. Her gaze was soft and kind, but also a little too perceptive.

"You love her, right?"

"Alice?" I joked. "She's kind of annoying and pushy, but yeah, most of the time I love her."

When my two friends continued to stare at me, I dropped the act.

"I love Camille more than anything," I admitted. "I miss her so much."

"Then you're going to need to do whatever it takes to get her back," Miranda instructed.

"I really hurt her. And...well, I never even told her I loved her."

"Why not?" Alice asked. "You've been together for what? Over four months? It's been clear to every one of us how you feel."

"I don't know. It felt like it was too soon."

Alice rolled her eyes but when she opened her mouth, Miranda quieted her again.

"Let's figure out a plan to get your girl back."

"I don't think she'll ever forgive me for how I treated her," I said miserably.

"Well, you'll never know until you try, Maddie."

# CAMILLE

Seven twenty-nine. Even though Madison hadn't come near the coffee shop since "The Incident", as I was thinking of it, out of habit I tracked the time until her usual arrival. I had been miserable the last three weeks. Missing the only woman I'd never loved. Missing my best friend. Missing Madison.

Then, as if I'd manifested her with just my thoughts, the clock turned over to seven thirty and the door opened. Madison came in, wearing a simple sundress and sandals instead of her usual attire. Her dark hair hung loose down her shoulders, and her lips were glossy with the pink gloss that I knew tasted like watermelon. Not her usual weekday attire.

She walked up to the counter, her eyes soft and questioning, and I steeled myself. I didn't know why she was here, but there was no way I was going to let her hurt me more than she already had. I'd been through hell because of her, and there was no way I was going back.

"Your usual?" I asked curtly.

Madison shook her head. "I want something different this morning please."

I raised my eyebrows in surprise. In all these months, Madison had never varied her order. Not once. When she continued to stare at me, I waved my hand impatiently, wanting to get this little visit over as quickly as possible.

"Well, what do you want?"

She slid a key onto the counter. It was connected to a keychain with a tiny heart charm. "You to move in with me."

My heart thudded but I kept my gaze stern. "Why would I move in with you after you dumped me?"

"Camille, I'm so so sorry about how I treated you. I know you were trying to help me, but I was so fucked up, I wasn't thinking clearly. Please forgive me."

She looked earnest and God knows I wasn't one to hold a grudge but then again, I also wasn't one to make the same mistake twice.

"Fine. I forgive you. Now order coffee or move along." I pointed behind her. "There are a lot of people waiting."

"Camille, I love you."

I'd waited months for Madison to be ready to say that. My heart thudded again but I ignored it, remembering the cold way she'd broken up with me. I didn't think I'd ever recover from receiving that text.

"Please go before I get in trouble with my boss."

"I am your boss."

"What are you talking about?"

"I bought Morning Jolt."

I stared at her for a long moment, then someone cleared their throat, reminding me about the long line of people behind her. I opened the swinging door to the kitchen where my coworkers were making pastries.

"Janet. Bob. Can I get a little help out here please?"

Madison moved to the side while the three of us made our way through the line. When the last person was helped, Bob went over to stand in front of Madison.

"It's a pleasure to see you again Ms. Phoenix. I'm Bob Andrews, the manager here. I heard this morning that you purchased Morning Jolt from Mr. Jenkins. I hope this isn't impertinent of me, but I really hope that you'll keep the team on, it's a good one. They're all hard workers."

My boss seemed a little nervous, but Madison put him at ease with a friendly smile. "I've been coming to this shop for a couple of years Bob, and I know how great your team is. You have nothing to worry about."

Bob looked relieved.

"I wonder if you could do me a favor though?"

"Anything Ms. Phoenix."

"Could you call someone in to cover the rest of Camille's shift? She and I need to chat, privately."

Bob looked from me to Madison curiously, then nodded. "Yes ma'am I'll do that right now."

He turned to me. "Camille, you're off the schedule for the rest of the day."

"But…"

"Sorry, you heard the boss."

He gave me a little smile that told me that he knew something was going on between me and Madison and was happy to play matchmaker.

"Go on now, get out of here."

I sighed and stalked back behind the counter to remove my apron and grab my purse. Madison opened the door for me, gesturing towards the long black limousine parked in front of the store. I rolled my eyes.

"Again with the limo?"

"It's a special occasion."

We were both quiet on the way back to Madison's house. The scent of her bodywash filled the air in the small space and my nipples hardened, remembering the times we'd showered together. Let's just say we'd made good use of the detachable showerhead in her townhouse.

When we got to her place I followed Madison inside without a word, curious about how she was going to play this. She walked quickly, her cute little sundress floating around her legs.

"I need to show you something in my bedroom."

"Oh, I've seen what's in your bedroom," I snarked.

She grabbed my hand, pulling me behind her up the stairs. I'd never seen this pushy side of Madison.

I walked in and looked around the bedroom, surprised at the change in the space. The formerly white walls were now painted a soft purple, and a new bed was in the center of the room, one with a wrought iron headboard and a larger sized mattress. The bed was covered in a new gray comforter, a stack of multi-colored pillows against the headboard. A darker purple loveseat and chair, both with a geometric pattern in the fabric, sat near the window, separated by a floor lamp. A small coffee table was arranged between them, making a nice area for talking or reading.

She pointed to the two new dressers lined up side-by-side on the far wall.

"The one on the right is yours. And I cleared out half the closet."

"What's this all about?" I asked.

"I knew you thought the room was a little stark, so I warmed it up. For you." Her voice trembled but she continued. "I want you to be comfortable living here."

"Is that why you painted it purple?" I asked, surprised that she remembered my favorite color. I'd commented many times that her bedroom was too white, with the white bed, white walls, white rugs, and white furniture that a decorator had convinced her to buy.

"Yeah. I want this to feel like *our* room, ours together, not just mine."

"Our? You broke up with me, remember?"

She walked closer, her heart in her eyes. "I want a second chance."

"What if I don't want to give you a second chance?"

"I guess I'll just keep on trying."

I nodded. "And buying the coffee shop, what was that all about?"

"I heard the owner was secretly shopping it around. I didn't want some corporate assholes swooping in and ruining it."

"So, this is all about you keeping your favorite cappuccino?"

"This is all about me keeping you. I know I probably don't deserve a second chance Camille but please, can I get one anyway? I know I hurt you, I know I treated you like shit, but I wasn't in my right mind, I swear it."

"And what happens the next time you're not in your right mind?"

"You have my permission to tie me to our new bed and spank me until I'm back in my right mind."

I felt a twinge between my legs. "I might just do that anyway."

"Does that mean you'll take me back?"

I pretended to think, even though I'd already made up my mind. "That depends."

"On what?"

"Are you still going to tip me at the coffee shop? You're my best tipper."

"I'll tip you in orgasms."

I wrapped my arms over her shoulders and pulled Madison close. For the first time in weeks, I felt the weight of my depression lifted away. Everything was right in my world again.

"It's a deal."

"I love you Camille. I promise I'll do my best to never hurt you again."

"I love you too. Now take off your clothes and get on that fancy new bed. I believe I owe you a spanking."

# EPILOGUE – MADISON

*O* *ne year later...*

"It feels weird not to be going to the coffee shop every morning."

I snuggled Camille closer to me in bed.

"I like waking up with you instead of a cold pillow," I said. "Besides, you can still go there to write."

Camille's royalty income from her books had risen enough that she had quit her job at Morning Jolt. We were still keeping it as an investment though. I wasn't kidding when I'd told her last year that I didn't want to lose access to my favorite coffee place. What was the point of being a billionaire if you couldn't buy your own damn coffee shop?

"I'm afraid if I sit in the corner writing, the staff's going to think I'm spying on them for you."

"Then use your office here."

We'd turned one of my two guestrooms into a writing space for Camille, so she didn't have to work at the dining room table anymore. We'd spent an entire weekend painting the space and assembling a new desk for her. Camille had refused to allow me to hire someone to do it, but I had to admit, it had turned out great.

She'd moved in with me a couple weeks after we got back together, and while we'd had our adjustments, it had mostly gone well. The dating app had been right that we were mostly compatible. Asking her to move in with me was the second best decision I'd ever made, after designing the software that had made me a billionaire.

Last week had been our one-year anniversary of dating, and we went on a trip to Hawaii to celebrate. Sitting on the beach watching the sunset, we decided to get married. There was no fancy proposal, no unveiling of a big diamond. That wasn't us. Instead, we made the decision the way we made every important decision: by talking through the pros and cons and reaching an agreement.

Then we'd gone back to our beach condo and Camille had tied my hands behind my back with my bikini top and fucked me with a dildo until I was so incoherent that I couldn't tell you my name. I'd reciprocated after I'd recovered.

With Camille I was learning to be a little less regimented and a little more spontaneous, and I knew that I gave her a bit more of the stability that she craved. We were a perfect pair, and soon we'd be a perfect married couple. And maybe someday...parents. It was definitely something that we were considering.

"What do you think about getting married in the park?" I asked. "Or maybe by the wharf."

Camille stepped closer and met my eyes. "Baby, we can get married in the backseat of the limo for all I care. As long as we're together."

"Hmm, let me call the limo service."

She laughed. "I love you Madison."

"I love you too. Now how about we retire to the bed-room?"

\*\*\*

Want to read about how Alice and Jewel fell in love? Check out "My BFF's Sister", available now at https://books2read.com/BFFsister.

**You can find more of Reba's lesbian romances at *Books2read.com/rl/lesbianromance***

*If you liked this book, please consider leaving a review or rating to let me know. Keep reading for a special preview of Reba Bale's lesbian romance "The Divorcee's First Time".*

Be sure to join my newsletter for more great books. You'll receive a free book when you join my newsletter. Subscribers are the first to hear about all of my new releases and sales. Visit my mailing list sign-up at https://books.rebabale.com/lesbianromance to download your free book today.

# SPECIAL PREVIEW OF THE DIVORCEE'S FIRST TIME

## A CONTEMPORARY LESBIAN ROMANCE BY REBA BALE

"It's done," I said triumphantly. "My divorce is final."

My best friend Susan paused in the process of sliding into the restaurant booth, her sharply manicured eyebrows raising almost to her hairline. "Dickhead finally signed the papers?" she asked, her tone hopeful.

I nodded as Susan settled into the seat across from me. "The judge signed off on it today. Apparently his barely legal girlfriend is knocked up, and she wants to get a ring on her finger before the big event." I explained with a touch of irony in my voice. "The child bride finally got it done for me."

Susan smiled and nodded. "Well congratulations and good riddance. Let's order some wine."

We were most of the way through our second bottle when the conversation turned back to my ex. "I wonder if Dickhead and his Child Bride will last for the long haul," Susan mused.

I shook my head and blew a chunk of hair away from my mouth.

"I doubt it," I told her. "Someday she's gonna roll over and think, there's got to be something better out there than a self-absorbed man child who doesn't know a clitoris from a doorknob."

Susan laughed, sputtering her wine. I eyed her across the table. Although she was ten years older than me, we had been best friends for the last five years. We worked together at the accounting firm. She had been my trainer when I first came there, fresh out of school with my degree. We bonded over work, but soon realized that we were kindred spirits.

Susan was rapidly approaching forty but could easily pass for my age. Her hair was black and shiny, hinting at her Puerto Rican heritage, with blunt bangs and blond highlights that she paid a fortune for. Her face was clear and unlined, with large brown eyes and cheek bones that could cut glass. She was an avid runner and worked hard to maintain a slim physique since the women in her family ran towards the chunkier side.

I was almost her complete opposite. Blonde curls to her straight dark hair, blue eyes instead of brown, curvy where she was lean, introverted to her extrovert.

But somehow, we clicked. We were closer than sisters. Honestly, I don't know how I would have gotten through the last year without her. She had been the first one I called when my marriage fell apart, and she had supported me throughout the whole process.

It had been a big shock when I came home early one day and found my husband getting a blow job in the middle of our living room. It had been even more shocking when I saw the fresh young face at the other end of that blow job.

"What the fuck are you doing?" I had screeched, startling them both out of their sex stupor. "You're getting blow jobs from children now?"

The girl had looked up from her knees with eyes glowing in righteous indignation. "I'm not a child, I'm nineteen," she had informed me proudly. "I'm glad you finally found out. I give him what you don't, and he loves me."

I looked into the familiar eyes of my husband and saw the panic and confusion there. I made it easy for him. "Get out," I told him firmly, my voice leaving no room for argument. "Take your teenage girlfriend and get the fuck out. We're getting a divorce. Expect to hear from my lawyer."

The condo was in my name. I had purchased it before we were married, and since I had never added his name to the deed, he had no rights to it. There was no question he would be the one leaving.

My husband just stared at me with his jaw hanging open like he couldn't believe it. "But Jennifer," he whined. "You don't understand. Let me explain."

"There's nothing to understand," I told him sadly. "This is a deal breaker for me, and you know that as well as I do. We are done."

The girl had taken his hand and smiled triumphantly. "Come on baby," she told him. "Zip up and let's get out of here. We can finally be together like we planned."

"Yeah baby," I had sneered. "I'll box up your stuff. It'll be in the hallway tomorrow. Pick it up by six o'clock or I'm trashing it all."

After they left my first call was to the locksmith, but my second call was to Susan.

That night was the last time I had seen my husband until we had met for the court-ordered pre-divorce mediation. He spent most of that session reiterating what he had told me in numerous voice mails, emails and sessions spent yelling on the other side of my front door. He loved me. He had made a terrible mistake. He wasn't going to sign the papers. We were meant to be together. Needless to say, mediation hadn't been very successful. Fortunately, I had been careful to keep our assets separate, as if I knew that someday I would be in this situation.

Through it all, Susan had been my rock. In the end I don't think I was even that sad about the divorce, I was really angrier with myself for staying in a relationship that wasn't fulfilling with a man I didn't love anymore.

"You need to get some quality sex." Susan drew my attention back to the present. "Bang him out of your system."

"I don't know," I answered slowly. "I think I need a hiatus."

"A hiatus from what?" Susan asked with a frown. "You haven't had sex in what, eighteen months?"

I nodded. "Yeah, but I just can't take a disappointing fumble right now. I would rather have nothing than another three-pump chump."

I shook my head and continued, "I'm going to stick with my battery-operated boyfriend, he never disappoints me."

Susan smiled. "That's because you know your way around your own vajayjay."

She motioned to the waiter to bring us a third bottle of wine.

"That's why I like to date women," she continued. "We already know our way around the equipment."

I nodded thoughtfully. "You make a good point."

Susan leaned forward. "We've never talked about this," she said earnestly. "Have you ever been with a woman?"

**For more of the story, check out "The Divorcee's First Time" by Reba Bale, available for immediate download at https://books2read.com/Divorcee.**

*\*\*\**

Want a free book? Join my newsletter and a special gift. I'll contact you a few times a month with story updates, new releases, and special sales. Visit bit.ly/RebaBaleSapphic for more information.

# OTHER BOOKS BY REBA BALE

Check out my other books, available on most major online retailers now. Go to at bit.ly/AuthorRebaBale to learn more.

**Friends to Lovers Lesbian Romance Series**

The Divorcee's First Time

My BFF's Sister

My Rockstar Assistant

My College Crush

My Fake Girlfriend

My Secret Crush

My Holiday Love

My Valentine's Gift

My Spring Fling

My Forbidden Love

My Office Wife

My Second Chance

Coming Out in Ten Dates

Worth Waiting For

My Party Planner

My Broken Heart

My New Teacher

**The Surrender Club Lesbian Romance Series**

Jaded

Hated

Fated

Saved

Caged

Dared

***The Sapphic Security Series***

Guarding the Senator's Daughter

Guarding the Rock Star

Guarding the Witness

Guarding the Billionaire

**Playing to Win Lesbian Sports Series**

Tumbling for Love

Racing for Love

Spiking for Love

***The Second Chances Lesbian Romance Series***

Last Christmas

The Summer I Fell in Love

Snowed in With You

My Kind of Girl

***Menage Romances***

Pie Promises

Tornado Warning

Summer in Paradise

Life of the Mardi

Bases Loaded

Two for One Deal

Penalty Box

Rock My Heart

**The Unexpectedly Mine Series**

Sinful Desires

Taken by Surprise

Just One Night

Forbidden Desires

Spanking & Sprinkles

**Hotwife Erotic Romances**

Hotwife in the Woods

Hotwife on the Beach

Hotwife Under the Tree

A Hotwife's Retreat

Hot Wife Happy Life

*Want a free book? Just join my newsletter at https:// books.rebabale.com/lesbian. You'll be the first to hear about new releases, special sales, and free offers.*

# ABOUT REBA BALE

Reba Bale writes erotic romance, lesbian romance, menage romance, & the spicy stories you want to read on a cold winter's night.

She lives in the Northwest with her family and two very spoiled dogs. When Reba is not writing she is reading the same naughty stories she likes to write.

For all of Reba's stories visit her webpage at https://books2read.com/rebabale.

You can also follow Reba on Ream and Medium for free stories, bonus epilogues and more. You can hear all about new releases and special sales by joining Reba's mailing list at *https://books.rebabale.com/lesbianromance*

Printed in Great Britain
by Amazon

53029420R00059